Sticking Together

By **Diana Noonan**

Illustrated by Colby Heppell

Pearson Australia
(a division of Pearson Australia Group Pty Ltd)
707 Collins Street, Melbourne, Victoria 3008
PO Box 23360, Melbourne, Victoria 8012
www.pearson.com.au

First published 2010 by Pearson Australia
2019 2018 2017 2016
10 9 8 7 6 5 4 3 2

Publisher: Simone Calderwood
Illustrator: Colby Heppell
Editor: Steve Dobney
Designer: Jennifer Johnston
Copyright & Pictures Editor: Michelle Jellett
Project Editor: Aisling Coughlan
Production Controller: Claire Henry
Printed in Australia by the SOS Print + Media Group

ISBN 978 1 4425 2725 6

Pearson Australia Group Pty Ltd ABN 40 004 245 943

Contents

Chapter 1

What a Disaster—No TV, No Video Games

I **REMEMBER THE EXACT DAY,** minute and second that Dylan and I decided to train for the school cross-country run. It was such a weird thing to do because we'd never been really sporty. Sure, we went to the park after school sometimes to kick a ball around, but it wasn't like we were in a team or anything. In fact, we usually tried to avoid anything that meant putting one foot in front of the other in a fast-ish kind of way.

I'm pretty sure that our decision to start training had something to do with the fact that it was school holidays, winter, and we were **mega-bored**.

Dylan's mum had snipped the plug off his family's TV because no-one was doing their chores around the house, and my game console had fizzled out when my little sister Millie spilled her hot chocolate over it.

There was the added problem that Mum had got herself a marketing job and was on the computer twenty-four seven, so I couldn't even download some games. Whatever it was that got us started on running, the idea of training for a race suddenly seemed exciting. Well, at least more exciting than cleaning the car or babysitting Millie, which is what Mum said she'd make me do if I kept mooching around the house.

"How long before race day?" I asked Dylan.

He stared into space for a minute. "Well, there are two more weeks of holidays, and then the cross-country is a couple of weeks after we start back."

"Four weeks," I said to myself. "Do you reckon that gives us enough time to get fit? Five kilometres is a long way to run."

"If we train properly," replied Dylan, who suddenly seemed to know a lot about running. "I saw this TV show a while ago about big-shot marathon runners. They all followed these special training programs and stuck to them like glue—that's what made them winners."

"So we need to get hold of a training program," I murmured.

"A gym would have them," said Dylan. "Gyms have programs for anyone who wants to do anything. They've got personal trainers, too."

"How do you know?"

"I've seen the ads on TV."

"So, what're we waiting for?" I grinned. "Let's get down to Jerry's Gym and get ourselves a training program!"

"And a personal trainer!" added Dylan.

"Hey," I said, jumping up, "why don't we run there?"

Dylan gave me a high five and we took off.

Unfortunately, the gym we were headed for was three kilometres away. By the time we got there, half jogging, half walking (well limping, actually, at the end), we were puffing so hard we nearly fell over.

"You sure you want to do this running stuff?" I wheezed.

Dylan was doubled over holding onto his stomach, but I thought I saw him nod. "Come on," he said, when he'd caught his breath. "Let's go inside and find someone to talk to."

When the receptionist on duty at the desk finished listening to what we were planning, she looked at us as if we were some sort of algae that had just been scraped off the side of an aquarium.

"Sure you get a training program if you join the gym," she smiled, too nicely. "A membership will cost you a hundred and twenty dollars each."

I almost choked. Dylan must have looked a bit sick, too, because the receptionist added, "Actually, it's only a hundred and *ten* if you join this month—it's a special winter offer."

"How about a personal trainer?" I asked, recovering a little and thinking that if we had a personal trainer, they'd probably give us the training program for nothing.

"A personal trainer is fifty dollars an hour and you have to sign up for a minimum of five hours," said the receptionist. She was now so bored with us that she actually got out her mobile phone and started texting.

"That's … that's two hundred and fifty dollars!" hissed Dylan. "Come on, Bradley, think of something else. We've *got* to get a training program."

"Look," said the receptionist, obviously keen to get rid of us, "if you boys want to get fit for this race, why not look on the Internet for a training program? There are **zillions** of them."

"Really?" asked Dylan.

"Sure," she said. She picked up a scrap of paper and scribbled a website address on it. "Look this one up. It's great. It's especially for beginners."

"How come people pay for them if they can get one off the Net?" I asked.

"Beats me," said the receptionist, showing us the door. "Have fun, guys."

"Let's go to the library," I said, when we were out on the street. "You get fifteen minutes free Internet there."

"What I don't understand," said Dylan, as we started walking, "is how come she knew we were beginners?"

Chapter 2

Goodbye Lollies, Goodbye Chips

"OH, WHOA, wait right there!" I breathed. We were at the library looking at the website the receptionist had given us. "They don't really mean that—do they?"

Dylan and I were staring, wide-eyed, at the week-by-week program that had popped up when we'd clicked on "beginner" and "five kilometre run".

"It's not that bad," whispered Dylan, trying to calm me down. People at the other tables had turned to stare at us.

"But it says you have to train *every day*!"

"No, it doesn't," said Dylan. "Look, you don't run on Wednesday, you walk. And Sunday is a rest day."

"But you have to run up *hills*!"

"Really?" Now it was Dylan's turn to look worried. He pushed his glasses further up his nose and peered more closely at the screen. "Yeah, it does mention hills, doesn't it? … Actually, it mentions hills quite a lot."

"And what about *that*!" I gasped, pointing to the panel at the bottom of the web page. In flashing red letters it said, "Take junk food out of your diet if you want to be a winner."

I felt myself getting all hot and sweaty just thinking about it. Suddenly, it seemed like we were having to make our get-fit decision all over again. I looked at Dylan.

Did we *really* want to train for the cross-country when it was going to mean all this work *and* giving up lollies and chips as well? Or did we just want to muck around as usual on cross-country day and leave it to Linden Marcos, the lanky kid in our class who always won?

Dylan's finger hovered above the "Print" key as he looked across at me with a funny gleam in his eye. "You know, Bradley, we could do this. We really could. We could train, we could win, we could even get ourselves selected for the regional finals."

He paused. "Together, we can do anything."

For a moment, he sounded completely convincing, even if it was in a "Vote 'me' for president" sort of way. Then he burst out laughing.

"I got that line from a reality TV show I've been watching… about how to train your dog!"

"Can't you be serious for a *minute*?" I demanded. "We've got an important decision to make here. I mean, why shouldn't we be as good as Linden Marcos? In fact, why shouldn't we beat him?"

Dylan stared at the screen again, thinking. "Yeah, it can't be that hard … I guess. I mean, it does say the training program is for absolute beginners."

"So? You want to give it a go?"

"Maybe. Yeah … I reckon," said Dylan at last. "Yes, let's do it. And let's make a pact to stick together on everything: training, running, finishing the race—everything we do, we do it together."

"Okay, agreed!" I said. "Print out that program. Print two of them. Step one: we each pin a copy to our noticeboards. Step two: we figure out when we're going to do this stuff."

Walking home, side by side along the street, we felt kind of special, as if we were on some kind of important mission, as if we were already heroes.

We felt so excited about everything that we wanted to begin our training then and there.

But the program said we had to wear light shoes and shorts. Dylan and I were wearing our jeans and hoodies. So, instead, we talked about getting up at seven the next morning to begin our first training session.

"Isn't seven in the morning kind of dark?" asked Dylan.

I didn't get a chance to answer him because right then I heard the tune from the ice-cream van that roams around our neighbourhood.

"Want a soft freeze?" I asked Dylan.

"Can't," said Dylan, without hesitating.

"It's okay, I've got money."

"You don't get it, do you?"

"What?"

"We're ***training***, remember?"

"So?"

"So we're not going to eat junk food."

"Ice-cream isn't junk food."

"It is when you eat it as often as we do," replied Dylan. "So I'm not going to have one and neither are you, because we've agreed to stick together on everything."

I swallowed hard. As the ice-cream van pulled up around the corner of the next street, I deliberately walked in the other direction.

"This is it," I told Dylan. "This is the real beginning of our training. If I can say 'no' to one of Mr Vitti's soft freezes, I can win that cross-country no trouble."

"*We*," said Dylan. "*We* can win the cross-country. The key to success is sticking together—don't forget that!"

Chapter 3

Seven Is Too Early!

IT WASN'T EASY getting up at 7 a.m. the next morning to do the stretching exercises we were supposed to complete before going on our first training session. And it was freezing cold in Dylan's garage where we'd decided to meet.

"Twenty-three, twenty-two, twenty-one ..." chanted Dylan, leaning forward and counting down the seconds he was supposed to be holding the stretch. "Mm-mm, feel those hamstring muscles!"

"I didn't know I had any," I groaned.

"Right," said Dylan, jumping up and consulting the training program. "Now, it's out the door and walk one minute, jog two minutes, then repeat for twenty-five minutes."

"Twenty-five minutes? Are you sure that's all?"

"That's what it says," said Dylan.

It sounded so easy, but after fifteen minutes of the routine, I couldn't wait to stop.

"Can't we have a quick break?" I begged.

"No," said Dylan. "We've got to keep our heart rates up for twenty-five minutes. And we haven't come to the hill yet."

"*Hill*? What hill?"

We turned into View Street.

"Oh no!" I said. "You must be crazy. We can't run up there."

"It's only two minutes at a time," insisted Dylan. "And it's not running, it's jogging. Come on. We have to do it together—side by side."

View Street is the steepest street in town. It's so steep that they have a gumball-rolling competition down it each year, and tourists who walk to the top get a certificate from their tour bus driver.

Walking up the steep slope was hard enough, but when we had to jog, I'm pretty sure I was running on the spot. In fact, I couldn't actually believe it when we reached the top. My heart was pounding in my chest and I thought I was going to die. I knew Dylan was feeling the same. But for all that, when I looked back down the hill, it did feel kind of cool to think that we'd run all the way up there—well, run and walked.

I even sort of wished that we could do it all over again, right then and there!

"You've got the runner's high," explained Dylan, when I suggested this. "It's to do with your body producing all these feel-great chemicals when you exercise."

"How do you know all this stuff?" I asked.

"TV," said Dylan.

I was beginning to see why his mum had cut the plug off their television.

Dylan said we weren't allowed to do any more running that day, even if we wanted to. If we did, we'd just end up injuring ourselves.

"So what are we supposed to do?" I asked. "Sit around and twiddle our thumbs?" I seemed to have forgotten that we'd already spent an entire week of our holidays doing just that.

"We could cross-train," said Dylan. He smoothed out the training program and read from a little box that I hadn't noticed before.

"When you've done your quota of running and walking, you can do something else, like rowing, cycling or swimming."

"How about cycling *and* swimming?" I asked, and then stopped. Was that me who had just said that? Me, Bradley Eason, suggesting that we actually do *more* exercise than we had to?

Dylan and I spent the rest of the morning at the swimming pool. And we didn't just jump off the diving board or muck around in the wave pool. We aqua-jogged.

There was a free session starting at 11.30 a.m. and, apart from us being the only two in the class who were under ninety-five years old, it was awesome!

By the end, we were puffing so hard we couldn't even talk!

On the way home, we walked straight past the snack machine filled with lollies and went back to Dylan's for cheese and salad sandwiches—unbelievable!

We'd planned to go cycling that afternoon but by the time we'd had lunch, I could hardly keep my eyes open.

"When did you say that rest day was?" I asked Dylan, as we were lying on the couches in his lounge room. "Dylan?"

I looked over at him, but he was sound asleep with the training program lying on his chest.

"Forget it," I mumbled. We were sticking together on this program. When Dylan slept, I slept, too.

Chapter 4

New Shoes

BY THE END OF OUR FIRST WEEK of training, Dylan and I could jog for eight minutes without stopping. We were jogging and walking a total of one hour a day and then cross-training in the pool and on our bikes for another two hours. The aqua-jogging workouts were the hardest, not because of the exercise, but because a couple of the old ladies in the group had really taken a shine to us and were always trying to buy us chocolate bars.

Every morning, when we went out at 7.15 to train, we'd see the same group of people—men and women (some as old as my grandad) and even a couple of little kids jogging with their parents.

Whenever someone waved to us or called out "Morning, boys!" in a businesslike sort of way as they shot past in their running shoes or on their racing bikes, Dylan and I felt kind of important. It was like we were in a special club, and it made us move faster.

One morning, towards the end of our second week of training, we realised that we weren't just jogging, we were running. And, what's more, we were doing it non-stop for twenty minutes!

At home, Mum was starting to make comments like, "You and Dylan are really serious about this cross-country training, aren't you? Do you think we should get you some proper running shoes?"

Mum must have talked to Dad about it because when he came to visit on Wednesday night, he was carrying a box. Inside it was the most ***amazing*** pair of silver and red running shoes. I tried them on and went for a quick sprint around the yard.

"It's like wearing slippers!" I shouted.

Then an awful thought came over me.

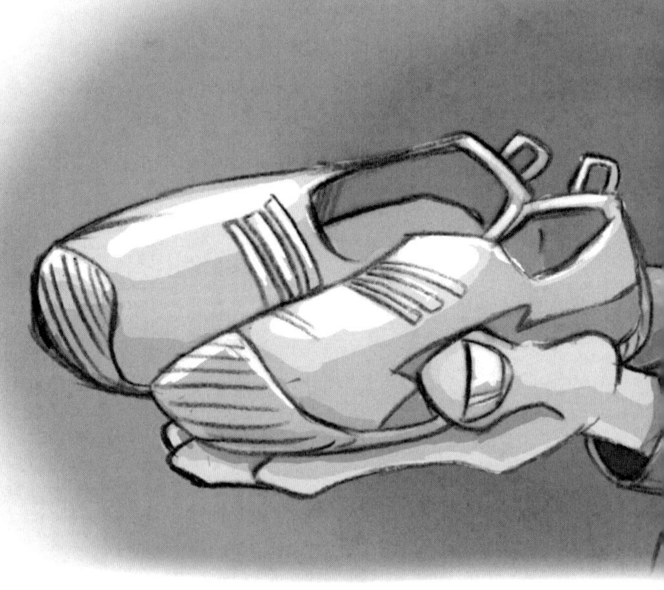

How could I wear a proper pair of running shoes when Dylan only had sneakers?

I didn't have to worry for long because, a few minutes later, the phone rang. It was Dylan. My dad had been talking to his parents and Dylan had new running shoes too!

Not everything was perfect, though. In fact, a couple of things made training a whole lot more difficult than it had been. The first was that our program took a major leap in week three. Now we weren't just expected to run for twenty to thirty minutes without stopping—we were supposed to increase our running speed from seven minutes a kilometre to six. That hurt!

It wasn't just our legs that felt tired and sore, it was our arms too, especially our shoulders.

Unfortunately, resting wasn't the answer. What we had to do was spend more time stretching, and that added an extra ten minutes to our training routine. It was at this vital point in our program that the worst thing happened—the holidays finished and school started again.

"Our bus leaves at 8.00 a.m.," said Dylan, who was hunched over my calculator doing some tricky sums. "We have to stretch for fifteen minutes and then run for thirty-five, so that's fifty minutes all together."

"It takes fifteen minutes to wake up, get dressed and eat breakfast," I piped up. "And then we'll have to have a shower after training and get ready for school."

"So we're going to have to get out of bed at ..."

Dylan's fingers flew over the calculator buttons, "… at, *oh, what*! We have to get up at six-thirty!"

We looked at each other. Six-thirty was crazy. Not even my parents were up at six-thirty.

"How about training after school?" I suggested.

"It'd never happen," said Dylan. I knew he was right. It had to be first thing in the morning or not at all.

"Our phones have got alarm clocks on them," I said, trying not to sound too whiney. "I guess we'll have to learn how to set them."

"Right," said Dylan, weakly. "You know, we can do this, Bradley. We can do it if we stick together."

"Support each other," I added.

"Yep," said Dylan, brightening up. "Way to go!"

"But six-thirty! *Six-thirty*!"

"I know," agreed Dylan. "Six-thirty *really* sucks!"

Chapter 5

Back to School

ACTUALLY, when you get used to it, getting up before the birds isn't so bad. And running in the dark with a torch on your head can be fun. We sure scared a few cats! But, best of all, Dylan and I were getting a lot fitter and a lot faster.

At school, our class was doing practice runs on the cross-country course twice a week, although "running" isn't quite the right word. Ninety per cent of kids were walking it or, in the case of Liza Munroe and Kylie Lucas, hiding in the bushes until the run was over. As usual, Linden Marcos was at the front of the runners.

Dylan and I ran all the way, but we held back on the pace. We didn't want to tire ourselves out for our workout the following day. Which was why it was strange that Mr Albeck, our sports instructor, asked us how long we'd been training.

"How do you know we've been training?" asked Dylan.

"You boys are looking good," said Mr Albeck. He slapped his calves. "Nice bit of muscle building up there. Shoulders looking strong. Been working out at the gym?"

I shook my head. "Just sticking to a training program we got off the Internet," I told him.

He nodded. "I suppose you know we take the top runners from the cross-country through to the regional finals," he said. "That's if they qualify with their time. Then, if they do well at the regionals, there's always the nationals."

"Yep," replied Dylan. "We know."

"You'd need to be running at five minutes thirty a kilometre to qualify," said Mr Albeck.

"Yep," said Dylan again. "We know."

"Good," said Mr Albeck. "Good work, boys. Keep it up."

"*Five minutes thirty*!" I exploded, once Mr Albeck had left. "We didn't know that! We're only doing just under six minutes a kilometre on a good day—and that's nearly killing us! How can we manage five thirty in less than two weeks?"

"We can do it," said Dylan. "I know we can. All we have to do is stick at it together."

Dylan and I had never worked so hard at anything in our whole lives—and we've known each other since we were babies. We stuck to our training program like glue and we put in a massive effort on speed. Even on hills we ran as hard as we could.

Some days it was like magic and I seemed to shoot up a hill like I'd been launched from a rocket, flying up and over and down the other side. Racing through the park, with the trees on either side, it felt like I was being swept through a green tunnel by a huge wave.

Other days, my legs felt like lead. It seemed as if I was towing a trailer full of bricks, and nothing I did would make the load feel any lighter.

But Dylan and I always encouraged each other. If he was having an off day, I'd let him know that it wouldn't last and that, no matter how he felt, he was still running well. If my alarm went off and I just couldn't face getting out of bed, my phone would ring and it would be Dylan with some stupid joke that made me laugh enough to wake up.

We were going well, and we knew it, but by the last day of our training program, we were still fifteen seconds over the qualifying time that would take us to the regional finals.

"I just can't go any faster," I said to Dylan. "No matter how hard I run, I can't do it."

I felt totally miserable but, as usual, Dylan had all the answers. How? He'd watched a TV program on this very problem, of course.

"You can guarantee that your speed on race day will be faster than any time you've done in a training run," he said calmly. "It's a well-known fact. It's the hype on the day—the spectators, the competition, the drive to win, the adrenalin …"

"The what?"

"Adrenalin."

"Oh, that," I said, not having a clue what he was talking about.

"Just relax, Bradley," said Dylan. "We're not just going to win this race, we're going to the regionals!"

Chapter 6

The Day of the Race

There's a limit to how many times you need to tie the laces of your running shoes, even on race day, but I was so nervous I just about tied mine into a ball of knots. I also went to the loo about sixty times in the fifteen minutes before they called us to line up at the starting point.

As we bunched up, I saw Mum and Dad and Dylan's parents standing with the other spectators. Linden Marcos was just a few runners along from us. My heart was thumping like a crazy drum.

Dylan and I looked at each other but there was nothing to say. We'd been over our plan a million times. We knew our strategy from start to finish.

We had just two aims—to run as fast and as hard as we could and, when we crossed the finish line, to cross it together.

"Ready!" shouted Mr Albeck. The world stood still. Then the **crack** of the starting pistol rang out.

My eyes were fixed straight ahead but I knew Dylan was beside me. We'd trained together so closely for the last four weeks that I even knew what would be going on inside his head.

We left behind the smooth mown grass of the sports field and crashed through the bracken at the edge of the park. We were already in the lead group of about ten runners as we entered the bush track that ran beside the stream.

"That's the way, boys!" called our deputy principal from the bridge above our heads. "Dig it in! Give it all you've got!"

Dylan liked that sort of encouragement and he started to run faster. I kept pace with him and we cut along the side of the track and took the lead. There was no time to say anything but we knew we had the edge on the others. We were pulling away from the leading group. We were even leaving Linden Marcos behind.

Out of the bush track, we leapt a low fence and splashed our way across the stream.

"You show 'em!" yelled Mrs D, the school office lady. "Go Dylan! Go Bradley!"

"Faster!" hissed Dylan. "Faster!"

For the next three kilometres, my legs didn't even feel like they belonged to me. It was as though they had their own plan of action and all I had to do was follow them. I don't know where the strength came from. I was still almost sprinting as we passed our principal, Mr Allen, stationed at the hockey field, and I realised that we had less than a kilometre to go.

In my mind, I started preparing for the finish, thinking about how Dylan and I had to make sure that when we crossed the line, we did it at exactly the same time to come in equal first. I started to say something to remind him of the plan but suddenly Dylan was pitching headfirst in front of me. I saw him hit the ground, like he was doing a forward roll, and then he was rolling over and over in the long grass and moaning out loud.

"It hurts, it hurts, oh man, it **hurts!**"

"Your ankle?"

"You go! Keep going!" shouted Dylan. He was holding his ankle and groaning and his face was white.

"I'll get help!"

"No! Keep running!" he almost screamed at me and then his ankle must have hurt too much because he just lay there, wincing and breathing hard.

I looked up, wondering where I should run to get help, but Mr Allen was already racing across the field and talking into his mobile at the same time.

"You okay?" asked Linden, slowing down as he passed.

"Keep going," I said. "We're all right."

I bent over Dylan. He was crying but I knew it wasn't from the pain.

"I'm sorry," I said. "But I'm not going anywhere, Dylan. We made a deal. We said we'd stick together and that's what we're doing."

By the time Mr Allen arrived, Dylan was sitting up and the last of the serious runners was passing us.

"You carry on, Bradley," said Mr Allen. "We can manage here. You finish the race."

I looked at Dylan but he was too miserable to speak.

"Okay," I said, beginning to jog slowly away. "But I'll be back in a few minutes."

Chapter 7
A Friend and a Coach

I DIDN'T KNOW that disappointment could hurt—actually hurt like a real pain. But by the time I was walking towards the first aid tent with Mum and Dad to check on Dylan, I had an ache in my stomach that had nothing to do with the running.

Dylan had tripped on a root, and his ankle was the size of a tennis ball. The first aid teacher was packing it in ice before Dylan's mum took him down to the hospital to be X-rayed.

"Sorry," said Dylan, when he saw me. He looked so sad it made me want to cry.

"It's not your fault," I told him.

"Right, let's get you into the car," said his mum.

"I'll text you," I told him. "I'll come around to your place as soon as you get home from the hospital."

Back at the officials' tent, Mr Allen was reading out the race results through a loudspeaker, starting at fifth place and working up. Linden had come in first and broken his previous record. He and Amy Jackson, who'd won the girls section of the race, would both be going through to the regionals. Everyone clapped like crazy.

I felt Dad's hand on my shoulder but, as he started to say something, Mr Allen interrupted the applause to make a special announcement.

"Unfortunately," said the principal, "two of our best runners faced a serious setback this afternoon. Dylan Johnson and Bradley Eason were in the lead by an astonishing two minutes. Sadly, Dylan fell and has been taken to hospital with a suspected ankle sprain." A murmur went through the crowd. "Bradley kindly stopped to help Dylan and lost his chance of a place."

Everyone burst into applause again and I felt my face go bright red.

"So we have not two but three runners who will be going on to the under-twelve section of the regional finals later in the month. Congratulations, Bradley, and good luck to each of our school representatives at the Milton cross-country meet."

Linden and Amy came over and shook hands with me while my mouth was still hanging open in surprise. When Mum gave me an embarrassingly large hug, I was too stunned even to complain.

"Can I use your mobile?" I asked Dad when I could speak.

He dug it out of his pocket and I ducked around the side of the tent.

"Can I speak to Dylan?" I asked, when his mum answered my call. They were in the hospital car park.

"Bradley?" said Dylan.

"Yep, it's me. Look, I know you're in pain, Dylan, but listen to this. They're sending me to the regionals. They said we were two minutes ahead of Linden before … before we stopped."

"Awesome!" said Dylan. "That's so cool!"

"But the regionals are two weeks away. What do I do now?"

"We look on the Internet for an *elite* training program."

"A what?"

"An elite training program. I saw this show on TV about elite runners and …"

"So we stick together on this one, too," I grinned into the phone.

"You bet," said Dylan. "I may not be able to run with you, but I bet I'll make an awesome personal trainer!"

I still had Dad's phone in my pocket as we drove home, so when it rang, I answered it.

"Figured I'd get you on your dad's number," said Dylan.

"What's happening? Are you home already?"

"Nah, but there's a free Internet connection here in the hospital waiting room and guess what?"

"What?"

"I've found just the training program you're going to need."

"That was quick!"

"We have to be," said Dylan. "We're going to be condensing a four-week program into two weeks, starting from tomorrow."

"But you won't even be able to walk by tomorrow."

"We both have mobiles," said Dylan. "I can do a lot of coaching by phone."

"Really?"

"No problem. And my first bit of advice is to get to bed early tonight because tomorrow, your wake-up call is 5.30 a.m."

"You're joking!" I almost shouted into the phone. But there was no reply. "Dylan? Dylan, are you there?"

"Five-thirty—sharp!" said Dylan, and the phone went dead.

Five-thirty! How hard is *that*!

Then I thought about it. Not as hard as not being able to run at all. If Dylan was willing to shuffle around on his crutches for the next two weeks just to coach me, then I was going to train and run for both of us!

Five-thirty a.m.? Bring it on!